DARPA

MESIAL

MANUEL PELAEZ

Darpa Mesial by Manuel Pelaez

ISBN 978-1-952027-96-3 (Paperback)
ISBN 978-1-952027-97-0 (Hardback)

New Leaf Media, LLC
175 S. 3rd Street, Suite 200
Columbus, OH 43215
www.thenewleafmedia.com

DARPA

MESIAL

CHAPTER 1

Zon's legacy before he passed away leaving everyone to bear witness the glorious fire burial, which released Zon's spirit across the plains of Africa with purpose and to be known as the protector of the precious animals and sea creatures from extinction, Zon's son (Whit) and daughter (Shu) are now spiritual protectors of the animals and sea creatures from going extinct worldwide. They are now the spiritual children of (Donkere here) the dark lords, and the forbidden underground cities, both can see how the poachers and hunters, involving many countries in the black markets, for ivory, skins, horns, anything can be sold for profits, the money involved in this underground industry is in the billions of dollars. They shall reach out to their great friend Izem (Marcus), to introduce Zon's vision and see if DARPA can help out with this global problem. Having heard of how successful DARPA was in Afghanistan. Absolutely no one knows more about land animals then Whit, he grow up among them as a small child, and Shu, is known as the queen of the seas, as a child she would make the sea her second home, both have special relationships with animals and sea creatures, as if they were part of their own family. Absolutely no one throughout Africa and beyond was more respected then Zon (the tribal elder), his vision was well known even among (donkere here) the dark lords and their forbidden underground cities. Both Whit and Shu (the son and daughter of the late Zon), will reach out to the undercover agent stationed in one of the villages as a member of the church members, monitoring rebel and terrorist threats in the region. To contact their good friend Izem (Marcus), who is the team leader scientist of the robotic engineering program called DARPA. To introduce their late father's long last vision, which Izem knew their late father's passion for the animals and sea creatures which were going extinct. The next morning both Whit and Shu visit the village, they were both greeted with smiles and hugs. Their late father's legacy is well known throughout Africa, when they saw the undercover agent they all sat down and started talking. The rest of the church members heard the great idea also. The undercover agent told them that he would be honored to contact Izem (Marcus) right away. They all went inside the communication tent where they can make transmissions to their good friend Izem (Marcus). The transmission goes out to the DARPA facility stationed in the state of Maryland in the United States of America.

CHAPTER 2

They quickly speak to Izem (Marcus), he was so happy to speak to them, the memories Izem (Marcus) has of their late father Zon are very favorable and legendary for his passion for the animals and sea creatures facing extinction. Known as the great protector throughout Africa, Izem (Marcus) quickly sets up a meeting with Director Jones, and Congressman Whitman, to discuss this entire situation with them and make arrangements for transport by plane for both Whit and Shu. The next day they sit down and discuss this amazing idea, making arrangements for a passenger plane to fly to Africa to pick up both Whit and Shu, bringing to the states. The plane takes off to Africa and lands near the village where the undercover agent, church members, and Whit with his sister Shu are located. By this time word travels fast throughout the continent all the representatives of their respected countries are in agreement that something must be done about the animals and sea creatures going extinct. It truly seems like if Zon's spirit is everywhere, and his vision is greater than anything ever witnessed. A small group is waiting patiently as the landed plane opens its doors, the undercover agent, and church members, hug both Whit and Shu, saying their goodbyes offering their blessings. Whit and Shu board the plane taking off to the states to unit with DARPA headquarters officials. Once the plane lands in Maryland at DARPA headquarters, the next morning a small escort takes them to the conference room where the entire robotic engineering scientists are seated, Congressman Whitman, Director Jones, other experts are there also. For instance, a top zoologist, biologists, other types of experts in transport technology, energy engineers, etc. This is an epic massive scale project that requires a global corporation among many nations, head of many regions, unlike nothing ever seen. When the meeting begins Izem (Marcus) vouches for Whit and Shu, explaining to everyone that they have special relationships with the animals and sea creatures. They show footage of Whit riding on bull elephants, rhinos, playing with lions, tigers, having gorillas as family, even the snakes have great respect for him. They also show footage of Shu riding on different types of whales, riding with sharks, dolphins, sea rays, almost every sea creature as part of the family. Everyone is simply overwhelmed by what they are witnessing, it's as if both of them can communicate with the animals and sea creature using some form of mental telepathy, which they possess at birth. After the delegation witnessed the footage they all decided to make Whit and Shu the leaders of teams of pre-military cadets that would run these magnificent habitats. The delegation made up of different experts in their respected fields, decide on the names that each habitat will be called. The habitats themselves will be a massive futuristic conservation amusement parks called (UNÍ-WORLD), inside each sector they will be named. The names inside (UNÍ-WORLD), will be as follows: (ARCTIC-SPHERE), this habitat is meant for cold climates, next is (TROPIC-JUNGLES), this habitat is meant for jungle type climates, next is (THE-PLAINS), this habitat are open lands, next is (RIVER-BASINS), this habitat are meant for amphibious creatures, next habitat is (WILDERNESS), this habitat has a massive amounts of forestry, mixed climates, and finally the underwater habitats are called (SEA ODYSSEY). Other special exhibits are called (INTO THE DARK), this display is meant for deep sea creatures, there's a lot of science behind these giant circular thick walled aquariums, with image enhancing technologies like (futuristic magnifying glass with bend lighting rays) to see these magnificent sea creatures in giant size, (ENCOUNTERS) this display is meant for the insects and arachnid families, it also has state of the art technologies (futuristic magnifying glass with bend lighting rays, for objects to appear giant size.

CHAPTER 3

DARPA latest futuristic technologies with military assistance if need be will be on standby, mostly all the technologies from the outer perimeter, using the (HEL) high energy laser towers stationed every 2000 feet or less, the fencing itself is an invisible web of laser sensors interconnected beam network with buffer zones. Separate housing units will be in assigned locations where the most advanced spider drones are stored, these drones are a marvel of future technologies, equipped with missiles and lasers, capable of going anywhere with spider legs, they are assisted by supersonic stealth futuristic autonomous drones, which are located in separate locations and do not need airfields to take off. The most advanced super soldiers are in different units, these robotic soldiers are equipped with missiles and laser weaponry, tank type rolling system bottoms built extremely tough. DARPA has used these technologies in Afghanistan with great success, all this will be founded by admission costs, expedition tours, provide employment and training to locals that live nearby, many donations worldwide, and is guided by an extraordinary dream from the late Zon.

A bronze memorial plaque will be placed at each entrance of (UNÍ-WORLD), to embrace Zon's great vision that is becoming worldwide. To salvage the animals and sea creatures that are on the brink of extinction, at a worldwide scale, it's the responsibility of the human race to take action now rather than coup with the horrific reality of only having a memory of these majestic animals and sea creatures everywhere. DARPA will use its latest futuristic technologies to protect this magnificent habitats from terrorist, rebels, poachers, exploiting these animals and sea creatures, for extreme financial gains in the black markets. These animals and sea creatures unfortunately have ivory, skins, and different things that are used in medicine, that's why they are at the point of extinction. The next concerns among the delegation is transportation within the futuristic conservation habitat amusement parks, how to power these massive structures, how to control the animals and sea creatures to keep from fighting each other, get other countries involved somehow without invading their national security concerns, costs of operations, separation of animals and sea creatures, etc. First thing on the agenda is transportation, in every futuristic conservation habitat amusement park there will be a futuristic hyper-loop train system traveling inside clear tubing throughout the habitats, interconnected traveling at moderate speeds.

Next agenda is the power grid, all these futuristic conservation habitat amusement parks and transportation from futuristic hyper-loop train systems, to cargo vehicles, transport vehicles. In hot weather climates solar photovoltaic arrays mounted on the buildings and sculptural canopy elements along the hyper-loop train tubing, designs will also draw power from tidal waves to generate over 70 percent of the electricity needed to power (UNI-WORLD), rainwater harvesting and passive cross ventilation are also woven into the designs. In arctic climates only the latest advancements in solar energy, renewable energy, wins turbines, and hydrogen energy will be used in the engineering designs. This is 21st century and a marvel of things to come, a breakthrough of dreams to come, a chance for humanity to undo mistakes and bring about a greater future. Next on the agenda is some type of control of the animals and sea creatures, a special weatherproof and comfortable collars that deliver some form of electrical shock, enough to deter any species from fighting and attacking each other. Next on the agenda is extremely complicated, getting other nations involved especially the superpower countries which have their own advantages technologies. Let's start with Russia, if they agree to participate we can all come down to some type of agreement that they can use their own form of DARPA, they have many advancements in robotic engineering and drone technologies, plus other security apparatuses. Next is China, if Russia agrees we have a greater chance for them to be onboard also, we can explain to them that it's for the entire human race to save these animals and sea creatures from extinction. This will also give nations the opportunities to use their latest technologies in real time. The allies of the United States will surely be onboard with this incredible dream, this entire vision will become a worldwide effort. Next is the massive costs of operations, an endless list of expedition tours will pay in advance for studies and research year round, scientists worldwide are very interested, not to mention the tourist worldwide booking in advance also. These facilities will be state of the art in every sector, the most advanced and sophisticated advancements, never seen before by anyone. Next is the separation of the animals and sea creatures, in every habitat the temperatures are natural to accommodate the animals exactly like in the wild. The sea creatures same thing but more protected waters to deter hunting and game fishing especially commercial fishing netting. Food source will become more civilized, using fishing farms, designed areas for fishing, monitoring regions more to protect reefs and precious ecosystems. After carefully discussing everything on the agenda with great success and agreements are made, the teams are given the green light to proceed forward. First thing for the teams of zoologist are carefully gathering the animals that are on the brink of extinction, composing lists and capturing them to be placed in every habitat. Second thing are the teams of marine biologist to carefully gather the sea creatures that are also on the brink of extinction, composing lists and capturing them or towing them to designed protected areas, some species cannot be in captivity but are given satellite tags to monitor them by the pre-military cadets, this will increase their survival especially among whales and sharks. Next are the teams of engineers in designing the vehicles that will be used on land and at sea, for multiple level purposes, everything will be 21st century designs. DARPA already has their technologies manufactured and battle tested. The transport engineers teams will start with the designs of the futuristic hyper-loop train system and terminals to be used inside the futuristic conservation habitat amusement parks. The toughest thing on the agenda is Congressman Whitman, Director Jones, and a small delegation composed of teams of experts to introduce this massive project to other countries like China and Russia. Financial experts are present also to introduce the financial planning of operations. These meetings go on for months carefully reviewing the plans and scale of operations, in the meantime, the teams of experts have already started on the designs of each habitats, and the development of (UNI-WORLD). Agreements on the countries sites for (UNÍ-WORLD), and the habitats are being decided by its leaders, governments involved. This entire operation is at a worldwide level, with many nations making contributions. After many months past, agreements are made on the sites for (UNÍ-WORLD), Russia and China are also on board, but they will provide their own security apparatuses. For Russia and China is a matter of national security, and their opportunity to introduce their own version of futuristic technologies in robotic engineering and drone technologies, among other surprises. The future is looking bright and it's all for a greater vision, our animals and sea creatures are part of our world to save them from going extinct, and preserve our eco systems. Next on the agenda are the regional sites where the habitats are carefully placed, the different countries involved, all coming together for a greater vision (UNI-WORLD). The following countries are involved, Canada, Siberia, parts of Alaska, parts of Africa, Madagascar, Australia, Costa Rica. Delegations and representatives from each nation will be in conferences months negotiating, agreements will be made among them. The security apparatuses will be decided among the superpowers, the United States, Russia, China. Next on the agenda, first are the land animals that will be placed in each habitat, which are at the brink of extinction and are the rarest in the entire world. Next will be the birds, both land and air, these birds are also extremely rare, and at the point of extinction. Now we carefully switch to sea creatures, mammals, underwater breathing species, deep sea species, we must also include amphibious species.

CHAPTER 4

Let's first never forget why this extreme effort is being conducted, let's pay tribute towards the animals, birds, and sea creatures with their respected dates, that are extinct and will remain just a memory for the human race mistakes. West Black Rhinoceros 2011, Pyrenean Ibex 2000, Passenger Pigeon 1914, Quagga 1883, Caribbean Monk Seal 2008, sea mink (second half of the 19th century), Tasmanian tiger 1936, Tecopa pupfish 1970, Javan tiger 1976 unclear sighting 2011, great auk mid-1850's, Bubai hartebeest 1945-1954. After announcing this heartbreaking facts, let's begin with the endangered land species that are at the brink of extinction, according to their species determines what habitat they will be placed. There are currently seven species of tigers on the list, there are currently eight species of elephants on the list, there are currently seven species of bears on the list, there are currently nine different species of primates and monkeys on the list, let's begin with our albino species such as, raccoons, Doberman pincher dogs, squirrels and ground squirrels, reindeer's, pit bulls, Chihuahuas, cats, kangaroos, buffaloes, lions and normal, zebras and normal, gorillas, horses, poe's, short-eared dogs, cheetahs and normal, rhinos, now, we continue with our regular species, jaguars, javan rhinos, mountain gorillas, plains bisons, pronghorns, sloths, snow leopards, swift foxes, tree kangaroos, western lowland gorillas, dugongs, pangolins, saolas, Sumatran orangutans, Madagascar's greater bamboo lemurs, hirola (hunter's hartebeests), Sumatran rhinos, african wild dogs, amur leopards, arctic foxes, arctic wolves, black rhinos, black-footed ferrets, cross river gorillas, eastern lowland gorillas, greater one-horned rhinos, northern hairy nosed wombats, pygmy three toed sloths, red crested tree rats, elephant shrews (boni giant sengis), southern Asia's javan rhinos, durrell's vontsira (salandia durrellis), nelson's small eared shrews, giraffes, przewalski's horses, ground squirrels, Oryx's, red neck ostriches, Barbary macaque's, Barbary sheep's, Cuvier's gazelles, dorcas gazelles, hoogstraal's gerbils, European rabbits, red dears, sand cats, strip hyenas, western barbasetelles, addax's, hoogstraal's gerbils, occidental gerbils, Cuvier's gazelles, dama gazelles, Barbary macaque's, Barbary sheep's. Now, we move on to the amphibious creatures that are becoming extinct: There are currently eleven species of turtles and tortoises on the list, let's continue with our albino species such as, frogs and normal, alligators and crocodiles, lizards, komodo dragons, boa snakes, now, we continue with our regular species, Ecuador's rio pescado stub foot toads, rock iguanas, luristan newts (Kaiser's spotted newts), Tarzan's chameleons from Madagascar, Mississippi's dusky gopher frogs, Singapore's freshwater crabs, leaf scaled sea-snakes, hippopotamus, marine iguanas, poison dart frogs, horseshoe crabs, brongersma's toads, Moroccan midwife toads, North African fire salamanders, sharp-ribbed salamanders, varaldi's spade foot toads, let's include our list of reptiles that are housed separately, atlas day geckos, atlas dwarf lizards, atlas dwarf vipers, banded toed geckos, blanc's sand racers, desert monitors, Moorish vipers,

Moroccan three-toed skinks, mountain skinks, green psammodromuses, lataste's vipers, manuel's skinks, Doumergue's fringe-fingered lizards, Doumergue's skinks, ebner's skinks, false smooth snakes, small three toed skinks, two fingered skinks, We now move on to the rarest birds that are at the brink of extinction: let's begin with our albino species such as, crows, peacocks and normal, owls, hummingbirds, cardinal birds, now, we continue with our regular species mockingbirds, bald ibis from the north, rare araripe manakins, spoon billed sandpipers, Madagascar's pochards, greater sage-grouses, macaws, mountain plovers, tufted puffins, audouin's gulls, Balearic shear water birds, black tailed godwits, buff-breasted sandpipers, dartford warblers, eastern imperial eagles, Egyptians vultures, Eurasian curlews, Eurasian peregrine Falcons, fea's petrels, ferruginous ducks, great bustards, greater spotted eagles, houbara bustards, lappet-faced vultures, lesser flamingos, lesser kestrels, little bustards, marbled teals, northern bald ibises, saker falcons, slender billed curlews, sociable lapwings, white-headed ducks, yelkouans, let's include bats that actually are mammals but housed separately, there are currently ten species of bats on the list.

CHAPTER 5

We now introduce are special exhibits, starting with (ENCOUNTERS), this display requires special enclosures that has futuristic magnifying glass with bend lighting rays throughout,(which makes images appear giant size). This display is meant for insects and arachnid families that are extremely rare and are going extinct, let's begin with the albino species such as, tarantulas, snails, ladybugs, praying mantises, grasshoppers, now, let's continue with our regular species, bubble bees, gooty tarantulas (metallic tarantulas), Brazilian actinote zikanis, Brazil's parides burchellanuses, rare franklin's bumblebees, baishan firs, Amani flatwing monarch butterflies, black-legged scorpion (Opistophthalmus Fuscipes), acilius duvergeri's, atlas golden rings, calopteryx exul's, cerambyx longicorns, chalepoxenus trameri's, chalepoxenus brunneuses, onychogomphus costae's, orange-spotted emeralds, rosalia longicoms, southern damselflies, let's include some plants, Saharan cypresses , dragon trees. Now we carefully move on to our aquatic creatures, starting with our special exhibit called (INTO THE DARK), the science behind this aquarium is extraordinary, it's the 21st century technologies for everyone to see, the solution to is amazing display is as follows: hydrothermal vents (the actual vents on the ocean floor shoot hot water that attracts marine life). The giant aquarium water is about 60•F and added a hot jet, a water pump raises the pressure to 3,000 pounds per square inch. Thick steel walls withstand the pressure, scientists feed the deep sea creatures using an exchange tube with a pressure lock and watch them through a strong plastic porthole. There are bend lighting rays throughout and futuristic magnifying glass, to make the deep sea creatures appear giant size. let's begin with the deep sea creatures that are endangered and are at the brink of extinction, gulper eels, big red jellyfish's, fang tooth fishes, giant isopods, frilled sharks, mega mouth sharks, anglerfishes, vampire squids, black dragon fishes, goblin sharks. These special exhibits are guaranteed to draw crowds year round throughout the world, now we carefully move on to our oceans.

Chapter 6

Now we introduce our (SEA ODYSSEY) underwater habitats, these exhibits are simply breathtaking, it is also part of something much larger. Currently 5% percent of our oceans are protected. With agreements among many nations worldwide these will multiply many times over, underwater species and mammals need great distances to strive and survive. The (SEA ODYSSEY) habitats will have many endangered species and will also have the hyper-loop train system traveling underwater in some areas inside the lagoons where it's possible to build concrete columns for support. The (SEA ODYSSEY) habitats will also have special underwater lighting to see the sea creatures. Larger parts of the oceans will be monitored by DARPA underwater technologies, (SEA ODYSSEY drones), we will carefully discuss the DARPA land and sea technologies to be used in (UNI-WORLD). First, let's talk about the endangered underwater breathing sea creatures that will be in the (SEA ODYSSEY) habitats. Let's begin with our albino species such as, stingrays, manta rays, sea horses, angel fishes, octopuses, lobsters, we continue with our regular species there are currently seventeen different species of sharks on the list, there are currently five different species of tuna on the list, uncommon common sawfishes, red-finned blue eyes, pacific salmons, mahsheer fishes, vaquita fishes, arapaima fishes, hump head wrasse, Tasmanian giant freshwater crayfishes, barbus reinii's, barbus paytonii's, barbus ksibi's, barbus issenensis's, barbus harterti's, black chin guitarfishes, blue skates, bottle nose skates, broad sea fans, bronze whalers, colitis Moroccan's, comb groupers, common guitarfishes, common sawfishes, Portuguese dog fishes, queen triggerfishes, rabbit fishes, white groupers, dusky groupers, European eels, giant butterfly rays, large-eyed rabbit fishes, large-tooth sawfishes, long-nosed skates, Chinese paddlefishes.

CHAPTER 7

Now we carefully move on to sea mammals: There are currently eleven different species of whales on the list, there are currently eight different species of dolphins on the list, rare vaquetas, galápagos penguins, narwhals, sea lions, seals, southern rock hopper penguins, dugongs, albino penguins, Mediterranean monk seals, Eurasian otters. Agreements among nations worldwide will reduce our oceans greatest challenges like commercial fishing netting, whale hunting, shark finning, dumping toxic waste, plastic products.

Chapter 8

DARPA technologies are the forefront of scientific breakthroughs, we will discuss the land and sea technologies that will be used in (UNÍ-WORLD), (SEA ODYSSEY), and our protected ocean regions. The future is here in autonomous technologies and DARPA is at the forefront of breakthroughs, let's begin with land futuristic cargo vehicles. Hydrogen fuel cells, fuel cells work by electrochemically combining hydrogen, stored in a pressurized tank, with air to generate an electric current, the only emission is water vapour. Hydrogen can be produced using renewable energy via electrolysis (using a current to separate water into hydrogen and oxygen. Hydrogen fuel-cell trucks of the future/ a platform with wheels that can be equipped for a variety of tasks, and could be outfitted for autonomous driving. Future generation of fuel-cell system provides electricity for electric motors at each axle, maximum range on hydrogen is way over 400 miles, it also has a supplemental lithium-ion battery pack. Now we move on to the fascinating world of autonomous underwater system drones, here the science is unbelievable. Let's begin, naval electromagnetic programs, including the electromagnetic catapult and rail guns. "Shaft less" rim-driven pump jet, a revolutionary and silent propulsion system, run on a medium-voltage, direct-current system. Integrated electrical propulsion system (IEPS), turns all the output of the engine into electricity, the high electrical output can be used to power motors for the propellers or potentially high-energy weapons. Renewable hydrogen for use in fuel cells, one-shot system that extracts hydrogen from seawater, with the added bonus of capturing carbon dioxide, creating hydrocarbon fuels. Designated snack areas are displayed throughout (UNÍ-WORLD), futuristic recycling trash towers are posted, all materials are made from special plastics that when put into the trash towers a special light beaming inside turns plastic into liquid. Everything is carefully filtered food is turned into organic materials for plant growth, plastic is liquefied flows in pipes underground to a nearby station where it can be molded into any shape, folks, spoons, knives, plates, cups, trays, and even napkins a mixture of plastic and paper. State of the art technologies are displayed throughout (UNÍ-WORLD), bringing solutions to global problems. Construction begins making (UNI-WORLD), a reality and the habitats, construction will be done by crews rotating around the clock in 24 hour cycles. The investors, the donations, are pouring in at a global level for this magnificent dream, the tours are sold out around the years. This achievement is mankind's greatest moments, and secures the survival of endangered animals and many other species for generations to come.

CHAPTER 9

Our oceans and the sea creatures that surrounds them will also be more protected, our precious ecosystems will flourish again. Marcus (Izem), has gone above and beyond to help out the late Zon's kids, Whit and Shu, after carefully placing them as leaders of the cadets. Whit will have a special uniform and travel only in some habitats with land animals that have bonded to him, for example, TOTO is a massive male bull African elephant that stands at 13 feet in height, weight over several tons, has tusks seven feet in length, in every habitat there's an land animal that has bonded to Whit like family. Shu will also have a carefully designed uniform for the oceans, and sea odyssey habitats, traveling with a blue whale called STAR, not fully adult yet but a gigantic specimen at that, they have bonded like family. As construction moves along, Marcus (Izem) announces that he is retiring, after the Afghanistan mission and his beautiful wedding with Julie the neurologist, Marcus (Izum) finds out Julie his sweetheart is pregnant, (they find out later on its twin daughters). Marcus (Izem), is set on having a family and enjoying life, after going through so many obstacles and overcoming so much diversities he has given more than enough to his country. The retirement celebration will take place before (UNÍ-WORLD) opens its doors, Marcus (Izem) is the leader of the DARPA robotic engineering program. After Marcus (Izem) retires the team of scientists which full names are Marcus Johnson, Jon Tan Lan, Sam Andre Dame, Tim Von Gleason, Ron Ben Ruckman. It is carefully decided among Congressman Chris Whitman, Director Jones of the CIA, and the team of scientists that Tim Von Gleason will become the leader of the team, Marcus's good friend throughout many years. Tim Von Gleason will have not only the other scientists but top zoologist will be added to the team as well. The scientists will monitor the habitats themselves, the top zoologist will monitor the land animals, and the cadets will do everything else. Top marine biologist will be added also to monitor the sea creatures, and over ecosystems, they shall be assisted by Shu nicknamed queen of the seas.

Chapter 10

By now, the word is out in the underground world, that their business which produces billions of dollars every year in the black markets, with things like ivory, skins, private collectors of endangered species, not to mention our oceans that is even a greater market with whales, seals, shark finning, and many more valuable sea creatures. The drug trade is also interrupted do to more ocean regions being monitored and protected by DARPA technologies. The encrypted message goes out to the top leaders of terrorist groups, black market investors, drug traffickers, top poachers, that only one representative shall attend a extremely secretive meeting. This meeting will take place in a remote underwater land cave, only top leaders shall attend, the encrypted code is unknown to anyone, this form of communication goes back to ancient times. The day and time is set, many things shall be discussed, alliances shall be formed, many topics shall be addressed, and a big surprise shall occur. A group of top leaders all gathered inside a remote underwater land cave with guards posted outside, the secret guess of honor was there already previously to their arrival. Dressed up in some kind of special robe, the top leaders are all seated on the ground like in a circle, the special guest reveals himself by lowering the hoodie. No one there can believe what they are witnessing, it's Terrence (Soldaat) in the flesh. After years have gone by, and everyone taught he was dead, since that dreadful day the military drones attacked the village camps where he was with groups of rebels and terrorist groups also. What nobody knew that everyone was killed except for Terrence (Soldaat), no one knew that when the military drones attacked he was underground in a special bunker reviewing plans for future missions? Terrence (Soldaat) went into hiding and after helping his brother Marcus (Izem), hide from the CIA operative hit squad, where his life was truly in danger. Terrence (Soldaat) begins his powerful speech, he grabs some dirt from the cave mixed with small rocks, and begins to say. We all come from the dirt we stand on, he releases the dirt onto the ground, and my heart was hurting for some time remembering my brothers in arms that died that late night in Africa. I saw their blood and body parts everywhere, I saw how they were slaughtered, I saw their spirits everywhere, I saw who is are enemies. Which late night past and the next morning I saw all the damaged inflected on our cause, on our visions. This has only made us stronger, more united, more intelligent, our brothers and sisters souls are with us forever, we shall stand together to fight these future technologies. We shall not allow these future technologies to take over many parts of our countries, many parts of our oceans, taking away our financial empires. We shall spread the word throughout are brothers and sisters for our cause, as if this day we shall be known as the (Secret Order), we shall be better organized, are attacks shall be well planned and coordinated, we shall do everything to bring down these future technologies. Our equipment, boats, vehicles, weaponry, shall be financed by rouge governments, which are our brothers and sisters. We shall rise up and show our resistance, our warrior bloodlines, and the spirits of our warriors shall be with us in battle. All our future meetings shall take place in remote locations, where future technologies don't exist or non-existent to function. The (Secret Order) shall be our code in history, we shall communicate in underground fashion, encrypted messages, let our brothers and sisters know that are cause is more alive than ever. All the top leaders gave a standing applause, envisioning greatness and witnessing this very spiritual day in history. After this memorial speech, each top leader are given their assignments, these assignments are carefully assigned. The assignments consists of the unmarked speed boats they need, these speed boats are super-fast with multiple outboard engines, painted all in black. The next assignments are the large caliber machine guns to be mounted on the speed boats, and armored vehicles needed on land. Next assignments are explosives, rocket launchers, grenades, IED's, serious hardware. Surveillance, layouts, of each habitat within (UNI-WORLD), are all part of the next assignments. The next meeting shall take place on the side of a remote mountain, we are waiting for the habitats and (UNÍ-WORLD) to be completed. Another agenda is the percentages of oceans protected, exactly what regions how many miles are protected. When the meeting is done, they all look at each other and say: may the creator watch over us and our brothers and sisters for are cause and vision. Now, the (Secret Order) has been formed and they all dispatch to their respected groups bringing their work assignments with them, and patiently waiting for (UNÍ-WORLD) and (SEA-ODYSSEY), to be completed.

CHAPTER 11

Meanwhile, construction is going as planned, the crews are working nonstop, a lot of progress has been made, everything is right on schedule, and the excitement is everywhere. Marcus (Izem) will be given one amazing retirement party, he will be given awards for all the achievements, the team of robotic engineer scientists, and DARPA officials are going to surprise him with everything. Many months pass by, and almost all the habitats from (UNÍ-WORLD) are almost complete, the (SEA-ODYSSEY) is almost complete as well, after completion many test will be required, once the teams of experts see everything is ready, then begins the transport of many endangered species. The transport of the endangered species will be done slowly and carefully, everyone involved in this amazing vision are so excited. After more time pass by, and with the construction crews working 24/7, finally (UNÍ-WORLD) and all the habitats are completed, including (SEA-ODYSSEY), the buoys are in place monitoring different regions of the protected oceans. The special exhibits are completed as well, (INTO THE DARK) and (ENCOUNTERS), these exhibits are heavily fortified. Next on the agenda, are testing all systems, including the futuristic hyper-loop train system that travels throughout each habitat, the (SEA-ODYSSEY) habitat the system travels underwater in the lagoons. Everything will be tested, including building structures, energy systems, the security apparatus provided by DARPA, has been battled tested in previous missions, with new frontiers in autonomous futuristic underwater drones, the futuristic buoys are also new technologies, working together with space satellites. After the teams of engineers, scientists, architects, and other experts, spend time testing and evaluations are carefully performed, all systems are a go and the date for the grand opening is not much closer. Now, the main tasks is transporting all the species to each habitat, this process will be done in parts with maximum safety.

CHAPTER 12

The transport begins, crews of experts with biologists and zoologists carefully monitoring everything. One by one each habitat is carefully being filled, first it's (Arctic-Sphere) this habitat is a cold environment, crews work around the clock 24/7. After some time passes the habitat is full, next up is (Tropic-Jungles) this habitat is a hot environment high humidity, after time passes by this habitat is full also. Everything is working like clockwork, next habitat is (The-Plains) this habitat is a mix environment, transporting species requires experience and expertise, after a considerable amount of time passes this habitat is full also. Next habitat is (River-Basins) this habitat is a mix environment, each habitat have complex ecosystems, mix environments, and everything is monitored 24/7 year round. After time passes this habitat is also full, next on the agenda is the habitat (Wilderness) this habitat is a mix environment, mostly cold. After considerable amount of time passes this habitat is also full. Now, we begin with our specialty habitats and exhibits, first on the agenda is (Sea-Odyssey) gorgeous lagoon settings which the hyper-loop train system can travel through a clear tunnel underwater to observe the rarest most endangered sea creatures on earth. After time passes is habitat is also full, the other parts of (Sea-Odyssey) are an increase protection of our oceans from currently 5% to over 25%, using high tech buoys transmitting live data through satellites. Since the larger sea creatures cannot live in captivity because they need a lot of distance and they are consistently moving, the purpose of (Sea-Odyssey) is to monitor those using futuristic technologies to protect them and ensure their survival.

INTO THE DARK
50ft(W) x 15ft(H)

The next specialty exhibit is a marvel of scientific breakthroughs, (INTO THE DARK) is simply breathtaking, this exhibit guarantees large volumes of crowds, carefully monitored by our marine biologist the sea creatures here live in a highly pressurized environment.

ENCOUNTERS
50ft(W) x 15ft(H)

After time passes this exhibit is full also, now, comes the last and final specialty exhibit, (ENCOUNTERS) this is another exhibit that is just unbelievable. So much science is involved in our specialty exhibits, the volumes of crowds are expected to be historical, after a considerable amount of time passes this exhibit is also full. The primary reason for (UNÍ-WORLD) and all its habitats, special exhibits, and (SEA-ODYSSEY), is to protect and preserve are earths legacy of endangered land species, amphibious species, birds, are special exhibits that displays insects and the arachnid family species, are deep sea creatures, underwater breathing sea creatures, sea mammals, to prevent an irreversible extinctions.

CHAPTER 13

The grand opening date is now set for (UNÍ-WORLD), but before this grand event takes place, preparations for Marcus's (Izem) retirement party has begun. Marcus's (Izem) retirement party will be spectacular, with tons of fireworks (in a controlled setting), the decorations will be breathtaking, everyone will be in attendance, there's going to be a state of the art children's play area, with every inflatable equipment, water sports, counselors supervising everything. This moment will bring the highest officials, colleagues, all the families together, this event will be remembered forever. Everyone at DARPA is excited, and their great colleague Marcus (Izem) will be greatly missed, but everyone knows the hardships he overcame and now he wants to have kids, and enjoy his life, everyone is so happy for him, but he'll always stay in touch. Marcus (Izem) will surely be missed, he did the honorable thing in helping out Whit and Shu, preserving their late father's vision, bringing Zon's dreams into reality. This special day has arrived, everyone is in attendance, Marcus is so happy, Julie is pregnant and everyone knows it's twin daughters, and Julie's parents, The Secretary Of Defense, Congressman Chris Whitman, Director Jones, the robotic engineering scientists Jon Tan Lan, Sam Andre Dame, Tim Von Gleason, Ron Ben Ruckman, and their families, the entire staff of experts in their respected fields, Whit and Shu, all the teams of cadets, many high ranking military personnel, father Mike, the sister nuns. The festivities started at mid-day but a full day of riding on the hyper-loop train system, looking at different habitats and special exhibits, time for eating, so many different types of foods, the kids are having tons of fun, and most important the security apparatus is extremely tight provided by DARPA, land and sea. Everyone is having so much fun, the fireworks shall be displayed in a designated area where it doesn't bring any harm to the endangered species. After the speeches, the firework displays shall begin, this day is made for Marcus and his family, and the DARPA family will always be a part of his life. The speeches begin, first up is the Secretary Of Defense, followed by Congressman Chris Whitman, then after that comes Director Jones, the robotic engineering scientists, many of the expert staff, some of the military personnel, Whit and Shu, father Mike and the sister nuns, the last one to speak is Marcus (Izem), who is in tears and emotional with gratitude. After the speeches the fireworks begin, everyone is watching the different color configurations in the sky.

Chapter 14

Meanwhile, in an unknown location on the side of a mountain, the (Secret Order) is holding its second meeting, the top leaders are summoned. The entire side of the mountain is completely secured, and similar to the first meeting (Soldaat) Terrence, is already there waiting for the others to arrive, one by one the top leaders arrive, when everyone is gathered. The meeting begins, (Soldaat) Terrence starts by saying, we are all here today united as one both the spirits of our brothers and sisters and the living warriors guided by the Creator of everything, we stand for a greater cause. Now, we check to see if everyone did exactly what I instructed in the first meeting. (Soldaat) Terrence, checking closely with each leader there checking if they fulfilled their assignments, first is the unmarked speed boats with super-fast outboard engines, the leader says check, second, comes the armored vehicles, the other leader says check, third, comes the large caliber machine guns to be mounted on the speed boats and armored vehicles. After carefully checking the first parts, (Soldaat) Terrence moves on to the other leaders, now, comes the explosives, rocket launchers, grenades, IED's, this part is given to his trusted explosive expert leader, the leader says check and tells him that they have boxes full of this merchandise, (Soldaat) Terrence, now moves on to his other trusted leader, for a full report on surveillance and layouts of each habitat within (UNI-WORLD), the leader tells him we have a overall acknowledgement of each habitat as close as possible without being detected, the leader says check. (Soldaat) Terrence, continues to say we have word when the grand opening will take place, but that day is way too predictable and DARPA's security apparatus will be tight that day, we will mount attacks at different points after everything settles down, it will be precise and with full force. (Soldaat) Terrence continues to say, secretly I shall spread the word on the exact day we will attack, after time passes we will have our next meeting in a underground bunker, to review our success and losses, this is our Creator's will. As always (Soldaat) Terrence speech is always extremely powerful and to the point, the top leaders now await the final word on the coordinated planned attacks. (Soldaat) Terrence finalizes the meeting among the (Secret Order) by saying this is a moment that will mark history, our Creator will be with us and the spirits of our brothers and sisters also, the top leaders applaud afterwards. They are dispatch and go to their regions to give word to the warriors under their respected commands.

C H A P T E R   15

The grand opening has finally arrived, (UNÍ-WORLD) has opened to the public, including tours of tourism, biologists, scientists in their respected fields, students from aboard in many nations, and domestic involving many states. Everything is well coordinated, broken down in groups, the crowds are at historical records, many counselors, teachers, guides, are within the groups. Everyone can read the bronze memorial plaque before entering each habitat, Zon's great vision: to salvage the land animals and sea creatures, sea mammals, amphibious creatures, birds, insects, arachnid families, that are on the brink of extinction at a worldwide scale, it's the responsibilities of the entire human race. The crowds are over capacity levels, but the hours are extended for the entire weeks ahead, every country involved is bearing the financial gains, every country involved is being saluted on a great size digital projection television set, naming the countries: Canada, Siberia, parts of Alaska, parts of Africa, Madagascar, Australia, Costa Rica. Also saluting every country's participation of species, this is a day that will go down in history. The monitors also mention every habitat status, (ARCTIC-SPHERE) full to capacity, (TROPIC-JUNGLES) full to capacity, (THE PLAINS) full to capacity, (RIVER-BASINS) full to capacity, (WILDERNESS) full to capacity, (SEA-ODYSSEY) full to capacity, (INTO THE DARK) full to capacity, (ENCOUNTERS) full to capacity. The world leaders cannot believe how successful (UNÍ-WORLD) has become, everyone is memorized, just how coordinated everything is. The security apparatuses are extremely tight, DARPA has state of the futuristic technologies land and sea, the other superpower nations have their version of DARPA also, and this provides in real time the demonstrations of technological advancements in many areas. The weeks pass by, with a continuation of historical numbers of groups, many tours have been paid in advanced, booked throughout the entire year, (UNÍ-WORLD) pays for itself.

CHAPTER 16

The cadets assist in tours, in every function of each habitat, autonomous futuristic technologies take care of the rest, and the main engineering scientists monitor the habitat environments. Whit and Shu, (Zon's kids) are more hands on, they each love to travel with their dear friends that are part of their family, Only in the habitats that relate to each of them, (TOTO) an enormous male bull elephant is always with Whit in some habitats, Whit also has friends in other habitats, he prefers to travel with his friends rather than using the futuristic vehicles, he also a specially designed futuristic weatherproof suit that protects him from temperatures, climates, etc. As for Shu she is known as the queen of the seas, her favorite way of traveling throughout our oceans is with her special friend and family (STAR) a gigantic male blue whale, not fully grown but almost 80 feet in length, she has a special harness to ride on this magnificent sea mammal, she also has a special waterproof futuristic suit, that protects her from anything like temperatures, pressures, etc. Shu's suit is so technologically advanced that it even provides her with oxygen, special lighting if necessary, she can keep track of time, a built in compass, maps, geopolitical locations. Nothing has been spared from providing them both the highest technologies from DARPA, and give them a sense of belonging to a special family, because their late father's dream is something special and will last way into the future.

Chapter 17

Meanwhile, while the weeks pass with unimaginable success of (UNÍ-WORLD), the word goes out among the (Secret Order) for the third and final meeting at an unknown underground bunker location. The top leaders have been awaiting very patiently for this meeting before the order is given for the massive attacks on all the habitats, that are durable and it's possible. The special exhibits like (INTO THE DARK), (ENCOUNTERS), (SEA-ODYSSEY), are almost impossible to penetrate because these exhibits are heavily fortified, to protect the structures and investments it took to build them. DARPA provides a heavy security apparatus and these attacks aren't going to be a walk in the park, expect heavy loses. (Soldaat) Terrence, is already waiting inside the underground bunker at a secret location, wearing his wearing special robe, under heavy armed security the top leaders arrive one by one. The top leaders take their respected seats on the ground in a circle, everyone is in complete silence, when (Soldaat) Terrence, stands in front of the circle and lowers his hoody. (Soldaat) Terrence, begins his speech, the day has arrived that our brothers and sisters who our witnessing this day from the Kingdom, our warriors who have given their lives to become spirit warriors, are here today. We embrace their courage and today we have all witnessed what modern technologies have turned our lands into, today we join our spirit warriors and plan the greatest attacks this world has ever witnessed. Let our Creator watch over us in battle, today we shall turn our lands back into what once they were, this is the will of our Creator and the will of our sacred cause. Every one of the top leaders were moved by (Soldaat) Terrence, speech and give a standing applauds. Let's begin reviewing the attacks, tables are in place with maps, geopolitical locations, times, points of entry, supplies to be used, equipment ready to mobilize, it's similar to generals and commanders preparing full range attacks. After carefully reviewing everything the day, time, locations, are set in coordinated fashions, the attacks will done early in the morning after the habitats open, they shall be with overwhelming force to cause maximum amounts of damage. After the meeting, (Soldaat) Terrence, tells the top leaders that after the massive attacks, they shall wait for time to pass by, and assess the damages and loses. The next meeting shall be after months pass by, and it shall be deep within the amazon, where civilization ceases to exist, things will be heated throughout our world. We shall remain unnoticed and in secret, the Creator is watching over us always. The day of the massive attacks was pure madness, at every habitat were under attacks, by land and sea, let's begin describing this gruesome day as it unfolded. First let's begin by land (ARCTIC-SPHERE), (TROPIC-JUNGLES), (THE PLAINS), (RIVER BASINS), and (WILDERNESS). Approximately, one mile by land crossing the buffer zone, the alerts are activated inside every habitat, triggering every storage units to open and launch endless amounts of spider dones heavily weaponized, only to be assisted by a mirage of supersonic stealth futuristic autonomous drones, also launching in separate storage units robotic super soldiers heavily weaponized also. DARPA also has (HEL) high energy laser towers every 1000 feet, plus a web of interconnected laser network that's completely invisible used to reinforce fencing perimeters. The entire DARPA security apparatus is mobilized and ready for battle, this massive technological force equipped with advanced technologies, is meant by an overwhelming force of armored vehicles with large caliber machine guns mounted on top, explosives, rocket launchers, grenades, IED's. The explosions are everywhere, just absolute madness, lines and lines of rebellious fighters, all in armored vehicles similar to tanks but smaller, with rows and rows of fighters ready to die in battle. This is happening so fast, no time to think just pure warfare, by sea it's even worse, (SEA-ODYSSEY) where the lagoon is located is heavily guarded, here the buffer zone is two miles, once any vessels pass that point the alarm goes off. Countless amounts of autonomous underwater drones heavily weaponized are launched into action, storage units launch an endless amount of spider drones into the air heavily weaponized also. DARPA air and sea technologies have many capabilities in warfare, by sea they are meant with brute force an overwhelming amount of unmarked speed boats traveling at high speeds, with large caliber machine guns, explosives, rocket launchers, grenades, IED's. The protected oceans are also under attack, the computerized buoys, the autonomous underwater drones, many endangered sea mammals are also being slaughtered. The explosions are everywhere, many lives will be lost today, this day will be remembered forever, these battles continue throughout many hours. Emergency protocol is activated, every habitat is closed, and the cadets in an orderly fashion put the civilians in protected shelters, designed for these types of emergencies. The special exhibits like (INTO THE DARK), and (ENCOUNTERS), are not any dangers, because these exhibits are deep inside the grounds of the habitat, and layers after layers of DARPA security apparatus are at the outer regions of every habitat, these exhibits are heavily fortified do to the extent of technologies behind them. After some time passes, explosions everywhere, even the military is dispatched for assistance. The rebellious attackers, used a strategy in warfare called hit with overwhelming force then retreat, leaving massive damage behind. Small groups of the rebellious fighters managed to escape before being blown up, and before the military arrived. Complete assessment reports are in motion, teams of cadets and military personnel are assisting in the reports. The aftermath of war are scenes from hell, horrific views everywhere, on land miles and miles of debris from parts of armored vehicles from the rebellious attackers, caused by massive explosions, mixed in the debris are body parts, gruesome scenes. DARPA didn't come out on scaled either, many spider drones were damaged, some exploded on impact, some robotic super soldiers exploded also, some robotic super soldiers were just missing parts do to explosions, some (HEL) high energy lasers were taken out also. The rebellious fighters on land with their armored vehicles, large caliber machine guns, rocket launchers, grenades, IED's, were not able to penetrate into the habitats, but they did cause damage to the terminals, shooting down many spider drones, taking out many robotic super soldiers, none of the supersonic futuristic autonomous drones were damaged, they travel at unbelievable speeds. In the ocean, it was also miles and miles of debris, covering the oceans with parts of the speeding boats, and parts of body parts floating everywhere, caused by massive explosions. DARPA also took loses too many autonomous underwater drones, and spider drones shot down. The rebellious fighters were not able to penetrate the lagoon where the special exhibit is located, but some endangered species were killed. In the protected oceans, many mammals were slaughtered, many computerized buoys were blown up. Whit and Shu are riding around with their best friends assisting the cadets and military personnel, a full damage report is being assessed.

CHAPTER 18

World leaders are outraged, Congressman Chris Whitman, Director Jones, and military generals order a worldwide manhunt on the criminals involved in these horrific attacks. These criminals must be brought to justice, the entire world depends on our success, (UNÍ-WORLD) will continue for futures to come, speeches are made live for the entire world to watch, trying to make sense of this isn't easy.

CHAPTER 19

In order to continue this story and the sequences of events to where we are at, I need to temporarily roll back time to introduce the next sequences of events and the origins in which it comes from. Let's go back to the beginning in 1958, NASA was formed, in 1972 is when DARPA was formed, approximately, a half century ago is when NASA launched two space probes. Powered by plutonium which is converted into electricity by onboard radioisotope thermoelectric generators (RTGs) which feed off the heat generated by radioactive fuel's decay. After leaving our Milky Way Galaxy, and entering the Interstellar Medium, let's do the breakdown of samples collected and transmitted. Interstellar space "between the stars" made up of clouds of gases and dust particles, where a lot of interesting reactions are occurring. Space between the stars is filled with atomic and molecular gas (primarily hydrogen and helium) and tiny pieces of solid particles or dust (composed mainly of carbon, silicon and oxygen) in some places this interstellar material is very dense forming nebulas, tiny traces of other elements such as carbon, oxygen and iron also exist. let's continue to examine space further and collected samples and transmitted data from the space probes, Alpha Centauri A and B, our nearest star system. Scientists discovered an Earth size planet in the habitable zone of one of Alpha Centauri's stars, a red dwarf called Próxima Centauri's (debate about whether Proxima Centauri's stellar activity has too much radiation for life to exist on its planet). Long after the space probes ran out of fuel and it's missions ended, they continued drifting into outer space, let's do a breakdown on space itself. Outer space is not empty-it is a hard vacuum containing a low density of particles, predominantly a plasma of hydrogen and helium, as well as electromagnetic radiation, magnetic fields, neutrinos, dust, and cosmic rays. The two space probes stopped collecting samples and transmitting data, it is not known how far the two space probes continued drifting into outer space, Heliosphere Oort Cloud, Heliopause. Scientists using space telescopes like the (Hubble Space Telescope) and afterwards a more powerful space telescope (JWST) James Webb Space Telescope. It is believed that some solar systems have hot Jupiter's or huge gas giant planets, others have super-Earths or rocky worlds between the size of Earth and Neptune, and it also revealed solar systems wildly unlike our own. The powerful space telescopes have given Earth a better understanding of outer space, let's breakdown the classifications, spiral galaxies (Sombrero Galaxy), SA(NGC 3185), SB(M31,M81)(M95,NGC 4725), SC (M33,M109),disk galaxies SO(M84,M85,NGC 5866), round galaxies EO to E7, M89, cigar shaped galaxies E6, M110 and NGC 3377, giant elliptical galaxies M87 Virgo cluster, irregular galaxies NGC 1313, merging galaxies NGC 2207, IC 2163 and the MICE, ARP220. Somewhere in deep outer space the drifting space probes are intercepted by some form of Space Energy Sphere. Both drifting space probes are confiscated, entering inside the massive Space Energy Sphere. The massive Space

Energy Sphere is made up of trillions of energy individual microscopic cerebrum molecules. After examining each space probe, which contains inside a 12-inch gold-plated copper disk consisting of 115 analog-greetings in 55 languages, and 12-minutes of music, images selected portrays the diversity of life and culture on earth. The drifting space probes intentions were to send a message to extraterrestrial life forms. These translations are examined by a higher form of intelligence. No one knows the origin of these higher intelligent energy type forms, where they come from, how do they exist, what are their intentions.

Chapter 20

The massive Space Energy Sphere turns from a golden glowing form of energy to a pitch black sphere. This massive Space Energy Sphere is about half the size of Earth's moon. In pure darkness and camouflaged perfectly to the background of space itself. It starts to travel at unbelievable speeds (warp speed which is approximately many times the speed of light), traveling throughout many solar systems. It is on the path to enter the Milky Way solar system and Earth. Since the massive Space Energy Sphere is so well camouflaged it cannot be detected by Earth's powerful (JWST) James Webb Space Telescope, which is capable of detecting anything many light years away, through many solar systems. the massive Space Energy Sphere cannot be detected by Earth's Hubble Space Telescope either. The speeds in which the massive Space Energy Sphere travels is nothing short of miraculous, it defies all human logic. Upon arrival into the Milky Way solar system and proceeding further towards Earth. The massive Space Energy Sphere positions itself on the other side of the Earth's moon, still camouflaged in complete darkness matching the background of outer space itself. The massive Space Energy Sphere suddenly opens up into four identical quarters, three of the identical quarters position themselves exactly around the Earth. Still completely camouflaged, the other quarter breaks up into waves similar to currents, into trillions of individual energy microscopic cerebrum molecules. The current waves travel completely camouflaged into the Earth's atmosphere penetrating all Earth's energy sources, nuclear energies, electrical grids, surveillance data, including televisions, radios, all forms of communications. Let's establish a timeline on current events unfolding, the space probes were launched in 1977, almost a half a century afterwards when they ran out of fuel and were drifting into deep outer space, that's when the massive Space Energy Sphere confiscated the two drifting space probes. Traveling at warp speed many times the speed of light they arrived exactly when (UNI-WORLD) construction was almost completed.

The three quarters positioned around Earth in total camouflaged have been only observing everything that is happening on Earth. The quarter of the sphere that broke up into current waves penetrating Earth's energy sources, is transmitting the current events happening on Earth, including the attacks on (UNI-WORLD) habitats by the (Secret Order). We are now exactly in the timeline where world leaders order a worldwide manhunt for the criminals involved in these attacks on (UNÍ-WORLD) habitats. The (Secret Order) forms another meeting in the sacred tombs which are underground at an unknown location after a significant time has gone by.

Chapter 21

The (Secret Order) has the severe numbers of their losses, and (UNÍ-WORLD) has cleaned up all the damages, cleaned up all the loss of human life, and repaired all damages on its hyper loop train system terminals. (UNI-WORLD) opens its doors once again, reinforcing its security apparatuses with DARPA, and military on standby, prepared for any further attacks, other participating nations do the same using their robotic engineering technologies program as well with military personnel. The three quarter of the spheres send telepathic messages, using different forms of communication, very low frequencies, sound waves called (echolocation), weak electrical signals, audible sounds, infra-sounds, signature whistle. Attempting to communicate with the land animals and sea creatures, no one knows why the three quarters of the Space Energy Sphere are closer to land animals and sea creatures, including sea mammals. The minute these transmitting forms of communications take place, Shu and Whit notice it right away. Both Whit and Shu are instructed to leave the habitats, meeting each other by the lagoon where Shu will be waiting for Whit when he arrives.

Chapter 22

Both Whit and Shu have special senses that are shared among their land animals and sea creatures, including sea mammals. Without any hesitation or contradiction Whit traveling with TOTO a massive male bull elephant directs TOTO to drop him off by the lagoon which is located many miles away. Whit and TOTO are like family, just like Shu and STAR a giant almost full grown male blue whale. Whit and TOTO finally arrive at the lagoon, and Shu is with STAR a special harness is wrapped around STAR for Shu to ride on, two can easily fit also. They both are given directions where to go straight to Washington DC where the Pentagon is located, they both know it's something extremely important. They both don't question the origin of the instructions, Whit and Shu have a special bond with land animals and sea creatures, including sea mammals. They both are riding on top of STAR headed towards the Pentagon, once on land there will be another form of travel awaiting for them.

CHAPTER 23

Meanwhile, the (Secret Order) top leaders are gathering at the sacred tombs underground, (Soldaat) Terrence, is already there waiting for them. The top leaders secretly start arriving under heavy guard, remember, the world leaders ordered a worldwide manhunt for the criminals involved in the attacks on (UNÍ-WORLD) habitats. Once the top leaders gather in a circle, (Soldaat) Terrence, has a bowl with him covered. (Soldaat) Terrence begins a powerful speech, we are gathered here today in memory of our brothers and sisters that have lost their souls in our sacred cause, here I have the lamb's blood which we will all drink from and unify our souls with them, he drinks and passes the bowl with large ladle (dipper) made of wood around, one by one they drink. (Soldaat) Terrence yells out, feel the unification of our souls joined together as one, overseen by the Creator, now, we are immortal spirits, our sorrow will only turn to energy for our battle warriors. Our next attacks will be more decisive and more intelligent, as we are dealing with technologies that are beyond our time. We will honor our lost brothers and sisters by being more unified and come up with other technics to secure victories.

Chapter 24

In the middle of (Soldaat) Terrence speech, the three quarter spheres that are positioned around Earth, energize themselves showing their golden glow, revealing their presence to Earth. Instantly, the military defenses of Earth and the nation's leaders are in absolute shock. Instantly, the inner communications among the superpower nations are relayed in military encryptions. The superpower nations put their strategic military defenses on the highest alert, (DEFCON 5), around the world Russia, China, NATO, all our on the highest alert. The International Space Station, takes many pictures of the three quarter spheres, but present no real threat to their presence. All the nation's nuclear weapons are pointed at the three quarter spheres. Civilians in the hundreds of thousands take to the streets with torches, flashlights, candles, thinking it's some kind of sign of beyond. The military from every nation mobilizes its military personnel's to restore order in the streets. Automatically, the nation's military and world leaders order all aircrafts to land, these includes, all commercial airplanes, helicopters, military jets, military drones. The order is also given for all submarines to enter ports, the purpose of these actions are because of nuclear missiles launched. These precautions are strictly made because of a nuclear electromagnetic pulse EMP, or NEMP, burst of electromagnetic radiation created by a nuclear explosion. Nothing is left to change, all precautions are followed by the book, since the three quarter spheres are already inside Earth's orbit, they are viewed as hostile. The Earth's superpower nations attempt to communicate with the three quarter spheres, with no reaction. The leaders of the superpower nations, are taken over by their egos and pride, their thinking process is the Earth is under some kind of attack. The leaders of the superpower nation's all coordinate among each other that it is imperative to show strength to what they view as hostile violators that have crossed into Earth's atmosphere in a stealth formation ready for a pre-emptive strike. This interpretation of hostile violators leads to the strategic military agreement among the superpower nations and their leaders to launch a total of seven hundred nuclear warheads into outer space directly towards the three quarter spheres. These actions are strictly for the survival of our Earth, countless attempts to communicate with these hostile violators have been without any response. The countdown is activated, by this time the hundreds of thousands of civilians are urgently ordered mandatory stay at home procedures. The streets are like ghost towns, everyone is responding to the mandatory orders, the countdown is getting lower. When the countdown reaches zero, nothing happens, the entire Earth goes dark. The superpower nation's military and world leaders are in complete shock.

<h1 style="text-align:center">CHAPTER 25</h1>

When suddenly some type of energy other than anything on Earth, only one main computer is on by this type of energy. Clearly on the monitor, it says in writing, BRING FOURTH THE TWO SPECIAL ONES, EVERYONE LEAVE. By this time Whit and Shu arrive with STAR the blue whale at the port of Washington DC, where two wild horses are waiting for them to take them to the Pentagon. It seems that the massive Space Energy Sphere figured how to translate languages, in order to communicate with the human race. Upon arriving at the Pentagon by horseback, Whit and Shu, present their identification cards to the military guards. The top military officials send word to allow them inside, since everything is dark, and nothing operates including cars, it's almost as if all the energies of Earth have been compromised, or taken over somehow. By this time the (Secret Order) go outside in complete darkness in total shock of what they are seeing in the skies above. All the civilians from every corner of the Earth, are seeing the total darkness outside and the three quarter spheres glowing in the skies above, even though the three quarter spheres are in outer space. All power is completely shut off on Earth, everything is stranded everywhere, from large ships, trains, cars. Even submarines drop to the ports bottom, the oxygen will last only some time before emergency measures are taken. It's a good thing that no aircrafts are in the skies, the International Space Station isn't falling from the skies, apparently, the Space Energy Sphere found no threat because it's a scientific station (for science research) not a warfare station. Whit and Shu enter the war room where the main computer is on, all military personnel have left and it's completely empty. The following communication is a combination of telepathic, extremely low frequencies, weak electrical signals, and short word written messages on main monitor. Everything will be broken down in it's entirely for a complete understanding of communication exchanges. Whit and Shu have a keyboard in front of main monitor to send back short word written response. Let's begin, (GIVE US A REASON), full translation (give us a reason why we shouldn't destroy Earth). Whit and Shu response (WE ARE NOT ALL LIKE THEM), full translation (we, meaning the special ones on Earth are nothing like all humans, even many humans are different then the majority). (THEY ARE DESTROYING YOUR PLANET), full translation (meaning the humans in charge of your planet are killing off all land and sea species, the humans are poisoning your planet also). Whit and Shu response (THERE ARE MORE LIKE US, WE WILL TALK TO THEM, WE KNOW WE LIVE ON A DYING PLANET) full translation (meaning, there are more like us on Earth, we will gather with them and talk to the leaders of our planet, we will address are mistakes and find answers to save our planet). (WE SHALL RETURN), full translation (meaning, in time the Space Energy Sphere shall return to see any improved developments, we are ready to transport your special kind). Whit and Shu response (WE WILL TALK TO THEM), full translation (we, meaning the others like us will talk to our world leaders to change for the survival of our planet, and we are ready to be transported when the time comes).

CHAPTER 26

After the exchange of communications, everything went dark, the main monitor went dark. In total silence, the trillions of individual energy cerebrum microscopic molecules collectively return to the three quarter spheres. The three quarter spheres join once again and the trillions of individual energy cerebrum microscopic molecules form another quarter sphere. All four quarter spheres join together forming one massive Space Energy Sphere, for now it's glowing. Suddenly, the massive Space Energy Sphere goes dark, camouflaged like the background of outer space. In one moment, the Space Energy Space disappears traveling at many times warp speed, leaving the Milky Way solar system. No one knows if any individual energy cerebrum microscopic molecules stayed hidden behind on Earth as surveillance to monitor future developments. The origins of these unknown technologies are beyond Earth's capabilities. In the meantime, Whit and Shu are debrief in the orientation room with top military command, which are directed with world leaders. Whit and Shu tell the world leaders that there are others like them with special abilities that are in many countries across our world. We are all instructed to talk to world leaders on how make the necessary changes to ensure Earth's survival. This entire process will take many expertise in many areas, we are now on a timer from many regions becoming uninhabitable. Are survival depends on it, we cannot continue the path we are currently on, the massive Space Energy Sphere will return. We all witnessed their unknown technologies and we have no answer to stop the Space Energy Sphere. The top military command, relays Whit and Shu message to the world leaders making arrangements to begin these difficult tasks worldwide. The main goal now is to send messages to the others like us by using telepathic forms of communications, extremely low frequencies, weak electrical signals, and sound waves (echolocation) if necessary. Afterwards, we will all collectively work with our world leaders around the globe to find solutions to difficult conclusions. The top military command ask Whit and Shu a question, how did the Space Energy Sphere found out about Earth. The Space Energy Sphere confiscated the drifting space probes we launched in 1977. The Space Energy Sphere have been observing us since or during the opening of (UNÍ-WORLD) and it's habitats, including the attacks. The Space Energy Sphere is somehow closely related to our land and sea species on Earth. The Space Energy Sphere can clearly notice how the responsibilities of the human race and its world leaders have dominion over Earth and our abusing that title. The closing statements, we shall all work together to overcome all the financial interest and gains from underachieving our comprehensive goals to assure the future survival of our planet.